The Little Merbutler

The
Little
Merbutler

Joyce Ellen Fowler Davis

VANTAGE PRESS
New York / Washington / Atlanta
Los Angeles / Chicago

Illustrated by Wally Littman

FIRST EDITION

Published by Vantage Press, Inc.
516 West 34th Street,
New York, New York 10001

Manufactured
in the United States of America
ISBN: 0-533-06282-9

Especially for Mark, Dawn, Matt, Misty,
and, with special love, Jim

Cast of Characters

Reveur (dreamer)—a little merbutler
Mermaids—sea women
Brut (rough/raw)—father of Reveur
Ami (friend)—friend to all

1

Once upon a time on the sea bottom, near the island of Whoknowswhere, lived a school of beautiful mermaids and one little creature. He was, and I'm sure still is, the little merbutler. His name was Reveur.

Reveur was the guardian of the mermaids. He was from a long line of merbutlers. His father, grandfather, great-grandfather, and ancestors on back to the beginning of time all had been merbutlers. Reveur was very proud of his job and the fact that he and his forefathers were the only ones of their kind. He and his forefathers had cared for and protected the mysterious mermaids—what a tremendous responsibility.

Reveur's father, Brut, had once saved three mermaids caught in a fisherman's net. He had called to his friends the dolphins, who came swimming at great speed to break the net with their powerful tails. Once the dolphins had broken the net, Brut pulled the mermaids to safety between some sea rocks.

As his father had in the past, Reveur had once risked his own life to save a mermaid who was being chased by a shark. Just as the shark had charged toward the mermaid, Reveur had swum forward, acting as a decoy, and barely prevented an attack by surprising the shark.

The startled shark had hesitated for a few seconds, giving the little merbutler and the mermaid a chance to swim swiftly to safety. Reveur's ability to think fast and act on instinct had saved them both.

Although Reveur was proud of carrying on the family tradition of taking care of the mermaids, he always dreamed of seeing the countryside beyond the horizon. Most of his duties, however, consisted of gathering seafood delicacies, collecting mermaids' combs from the sea bottom, and securing their underwater castle against enemies.

Reveur was also responsible for gathering seashells along a narrow strip of mainland just to the north. This beach was a fairyland of beauty, with mountains in the background rising up to meet the golden sunshine. Warm southern breezes drifted sweet fragrances down to the sea. Cheerful houses were nestled along swift, little hillside rivers.

As he carried on his duties, Reveur could hear an occasional train whistling along in the distance. Westbound trucks loaded with olives, bananas, and pomegranates hummed as they traveled up the hills.

The hustle and bustle of activity beyond him enticed Reveur to leave the sea for at least a short period of time. He wanted to travel the ancient highway and see the countryside beyond the mainland horizon.

Aware of the little merbutler's dream, the mermaids sent out a note in a bottle by way of the messenger dolphins. The note went to a special friend who made some secret arrangements.

15

Early one morning as the little merbutler was looking toward the mainland shore, he saw a large flatbed truck with a tank on its bed. The truck was backing down toward the sea right where Reveur was treading water.

Suddenly there was great excitement. The mermaids were swimming around telling Reveur about plans they had made and a trip they were about to take.

The truck driver was Ami, the special friend who had received the note in the bottle. Ami helped Reveur and the mermaids into the tank of sea water on the flatbed truck, and in a "flip of a fin" they were on their way. Ami smiled as he drove; he knew the dream of a lifetime was coming true for Reveur.

Because of their excitement, the hours melted together and seemed like only minutes to the little merbutler and his friends. Along the roadside, glimpses of sparkling ocean kept their hearts near home, while bright gardens of violets and roses danced along the mountain's side. Fresh, fragrant air filled their minds with a never-before-known freedom.

Suddenly, another truck loomed in front of them like a dark shadow. Screeching brakes and the smell of tires burning rubber turned Reveur's thoughts of his dream to cold reality. Unknown fear took hold, and the dream became a nightmare. Little tails were flipping everywhere, and water was percolating around them. For several seconds it was a turmoil. Then, as if by magic, the truck slid to a halt at the roadside, and it was over. Scared little faces stared at each other in disbelief, and a new feeling began to spread. Indistinct at first, the feeling began to build to a crystal-clear desire to return to the sea. Ami understood and before you could say "Mer," they were home.

What a thrilling adventure for the little merbutler and his friends! But now Reveur knew, after experiencing danger, that his dream could not compare to his real destiny of preserving the beautiful mermaids on the sea bottom near the island of Whoknows-where.